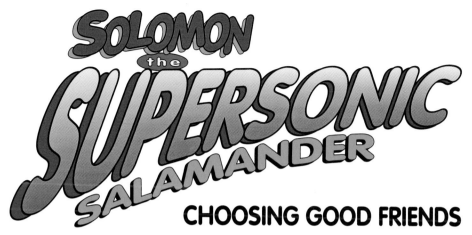

CHOOSING GOOD FRIENDS

Characters and Story by
Ernie Rettino and Debby Kerner Rettino

Design and Illustration by
Dirk Wunderlich

WORD PUBLISHING
Dallas · London · Vancouver · Melbourne

Illustrator: Dirk Wunderlich
Managing Editor: Laura Minchew
Project Editor: Beverly Phillips
Copy Editor: Barbara Bartholomew

Scripture quotations are from the *International Children's Bible, New Century Version.*
Copyright © 1983, 1986, 1988 by Word Publishing.

Library of Congress Cataloging-in-Publication Data

Rettino, Ernie. 1949–
    Solomon the Supersonic Salamander : choosing good friends / characters and story
by Ernie Rettino and Debby Kerner Rettino : design and illustration by Dirk Wuderlich.
       p.   cm. — (The Wisdom series)
    "Word Kids!"
    Summary: When a storm washes Solomon down stream, he meets some seemingly
friendly animals and learns from them and the Book of Proverbs how to be a true
friend.
    ISBN 0–8499–1017–X
    [1. Friendship—Fiction. 2 Animals—Fiction. 3. Christian life—Fiction.]
I. Rettino, Debby Kerner, 1951– . II. Wunderlich, Dirk. 1947– ill.
III. Title. IV. Title: Choosing good friends. V. Series: Rettino, Ernie, 1949– .
Wisdom Series.
PZ7.R32553So   1992
[E]—dc20   92–22866
                                               CIP
                                                AC

Printed in the United States of America

2 3 4 5 6 7 9 LBM 9 8 7 6 5 4 3 2 1

THE WISDOM SERIES

Dear Parents,

To survive in today's world, where there are few rules, our kids need the wisdom to make good choices. That's why we created The Wisdom Series and the lovable new character, Solomon the Supersonic Salamander . . . to help kids develop that wisdom. Solomon learns to make wise choices from a book with his name in it—the incredible Book of Proverbs.

One of the most important things kids can do is to choose good friends. Their friends have a powerful influence on them . . . for better or worse. The book of Proverbs is chock full of wisdom about that subject.

In *Choosing Good Friends,* your little one will learn right along with Solomon what can happen when you hang out with the "wrong type of critter" and what it takes to be a "real friend."

To reinforce the principles introduced in this story, we encourage you to read with your children the following passages from Proverbs so that they can discover for themselves just how *incredible* the Book of Proverbs really is—1:10–19, 2:1–5, 3:5–6, 3:7, 3:13–15, 4:14–15, 6:12–19, 9:10, 12:26, 13:20, 14:12, 18:24, 20:11, 22:1, 22:24–25, 23:17–18, 23:23, 24:1–2, 24:21.

We pray that the foundation for a lifetime of wise choices will be laid during the moments you spend snuggled up with your child enjoying the daring deeds of Solomon the Supersonic Salamander and learning from the Book of Proverbs.

With love,

Ernie   *Debby*

Ernie and Debby

Help!" Solomon yelled. "Somebody stop this thing!" It was stormy, and the wind was blowing hard. The lily pad Solomon was napping on had come loose from its roots. It was rushing downriver, carrying the pink and purple Salamander away from his home and friends.

The wind blew Solomon's green hair as he held on for dear life. The lily pad kept racing faster and faster downriver. Suddenly . . . THUD! Solomon's lily pad hit a log and stuck there.

The poor little salamander was a long way from home. He was too far away for any of his friends to help him now. And he was cold, tired, and soggy.

"Help! Anybody, help!" he called again.

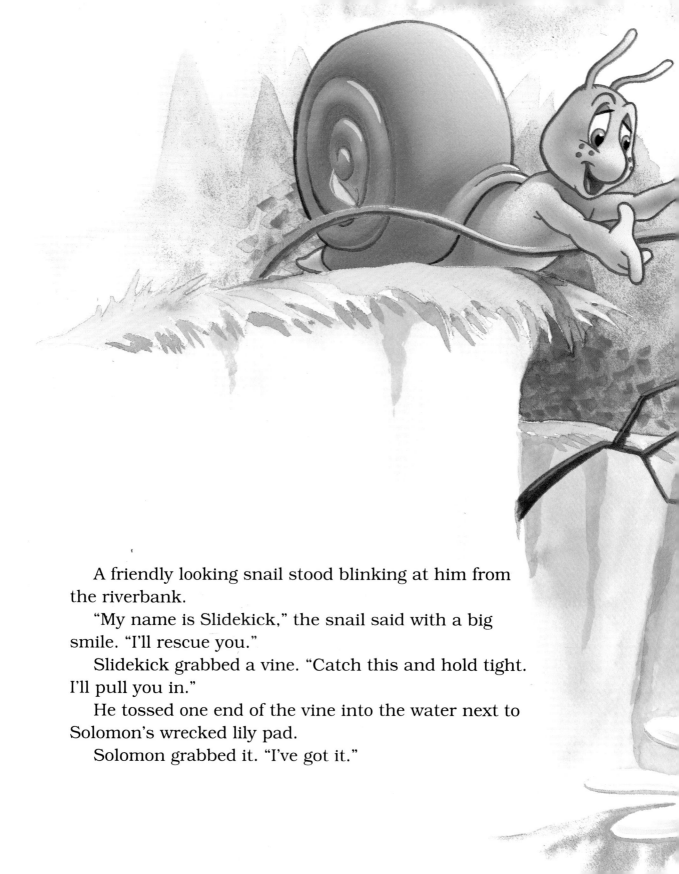

A friendly looking snail stood blinking at him from the riverbank.

"My name is Slidekick," the snail said with a big smile. "I'll rescue you."

Slidekick grabbed a vine. "Catch this and hold tight. I'll pull you in."

He tossed one end of the vine into the water next to Solomon's wrecked lily pad.

Solomon grabbed it. "I've got it."

Slidekick tugged at the vine. It started to move and then stopped.

"The vine is stuck on a branch!" called Solomon. "What are we going to do?" he asked, his voice shaking.

"Don't worry. I'll get help," Slidekick said. "Max," he called. "Hey, Max Magpie!"

"Holy guacamole!" a voice called from somewhere up in the leafy trees. "Hold on to your shell. I'm coming."

Solomon stared as a magpie in a big sombrero and a vest covered with shiny doodads landed on a branch above them.

"Caramba! You do need help." The magpie dived down to grab the vine with his beak.

He and Slidekick pulled Solomon to safety.

"Thanks guys," Solomon said. "I thought I was sunk for sure."

"I'm Maximilian, but you can call me Max," the magpie said.

"Caramba! Who are you? What are you?"

Solomon couldn't help laughing. Slidekick and Max were friendly *and* funny.

"I'm Solomon Salamander. I'm amphibious."

"Am-wha-bious?" Slidekick asked.

"Amphibious. I can breathe in or out of water. But the storm was so strong, the river carried me away from my home."

"I'm glad I was sliding by when you needed help, Solomon," said Slidekick. "We'll be friends that stick together closer than brothers."

"*Amigo* . . . that's Spanish for friend." Max grinned at the salamander. "*Amigo*, I've heard that name Solomon before. Back at my birdhouse I keep things that I collect. Like buttons, pennies, and other shiny stuff. Anyway, I found a book with shiny edges and your name is in it!"

"I'd like to see that," Solomon said excitedly.

The three new friends headed for Max's house, but they didn't know they were being followed.

The little bad bug, Bo Evil, liked to snoop around and hear other people's business.

He hid himself in the shadows near the edge of Max's birdhouse.

"Here it is, Amigo," said Max. "Your name is in the first line, '*The Proverbs of Solomon. These are the wise words of Solomon, the King of Israel.*'"

"Wow!" said Slidekick. "A king!"

"These proverbs teach how to be wise," said Max. "They teach what is honest, fair, and right. They help us learn to think."

Then Max read, "*Happy is the person who finds wisdom. Wisdom is better than silver.*"

Bo Evil couldn't hear everything Max said. But when he heard the words "*better than silver,*" the little bad bug almost fell from his hiding place.

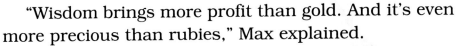

"Wisdom brings more profit than gold. And it's even more precious than rubies," Max explained.

"Awesome!" Solomon shook his head.

"Solomon, since your name is in it, I'll give you this book."

When Bo Evil heard the words *gold* and *rubies*, he laughed wickedly. "Solomon Salamander wants new friends. I'll act like his friend so I can steal that book and get the treasure."

Bo Evil was tiptoeing away when a loud chopping noise made them all look down.

A beaver wearing a long string of pearls and a big hat with a feather, was busily chopping down Max's tree.

"Mrs. Beaverton," Max yelled politely. "You're cutting down the tree with my house in it."

Mrs. Beaverton looked up.

"So sorry! I'm in such a rush. There's only one week left till it's time for my country fair. I had the amusement park finished: the Forest Ferris Wheel, the Willow Branch Roller Coaster, and the Bluebell Carousel. Everything was ready. But that storm ruined it all. Now I have to start over again."

"I'll help you, Mrs. Beaverton," offered Solomon. "My name is Solomon Salamander, and I'm new here."

Max and Slidekick also wanted to help.

Bo Evil saw his chance and jumped out. "I couldn't help overhearing. I'll help, too," said the little bad bug. Then he turned to Solomon. "Hello. My name is Bo Evil. I'm sure we'll be best of friends!"

"This is great," Solomon said. "I've already got four new friends!"

The whole gang pitched in to finish the amusement park. Max carried sticks and twigs to the high spots. Mrs. Beaverton sawed with her sharp teeth. Slidekick and Solomon hammered and tied things together. Bo Evil told everybody what to do but didn't do any work himself. Instead he played mean tricks on the others.

One time Bo Evil tripped Slidekick. Slidekick slid all the way to the end of the roller coaster track.

"Ouch!" Slidekick rubbed his bruised shell.

Bo Evil laughed. "Wasn't that funny, Solomon?"

Solomon didn't think it was funny. But he laughed a little because he wanted Bo Evil to be his friend.

But Solomon didn't know that Bo Evil had a plan.

The bad bug wanted to get everybody out of the way so he could steal the treasure book.

One evening Mrs. Beaverton talked to Solomon. "It says in Proverbs that even a child is known by his actions. The other forest critters are deciding what kind of critter you are . . . good or bad. You've been hanging around with Bo Evil, and he's up to no good! He's gonna rub off on you, if you don't watch out!"

Solomon felt bad that he'd laughed when Bo Evil hurt
Slidekick. "But, I want to have *lots* of friends," he
protested.

"Sometimes we want to be friends with the wrong
critters just because we're afraid of being alone," said
Mrs. Beaverton. "But God will be your friend, Solomon.
And He'll always be with you."

The next day Solomon walked along thinking about the bad things Bo Evil had done.

Just then Max Magpie landed in a rush. "Come quick! Pronto! Bo Evil's leading Slidekick to the salt pit!"

Solomon was scared for his friend. Salt would melt Slidekick! "That Bo Evil is no good! From now on I choose to live the way God wants me to. But how can we get to Slidekick in time?"

At the moment when Solomon chose to live God's way, something amazing happened.

Max stared in surprise as Solomon began to change right before his eyes. Only seconds before his friend had been an ordinary salamander, but now he was different.

"What's happening to me?" Solomon was as surprised as Max.

Solomon was becoming *SUPERSONIC*—super fast—so he could get to Slidekick in time!

"I'm *SOLOMON THE SUPERSONIC SALAMANDER*. And here . . . I . . . go!"

Off he flew to rescue his friend.

At the edge of the salt pit, *SOLOMON THE SUPERSONIC SALAMANDER* skidded to a stop.

"Bo Evil," Solomon said. "I'm here to stop you from melting Slidekick in the salt pit."

Slidekick's eyes flew open. "Melt me? Why?"

"For the treasure," Bo Evil said in disgust. "I had to get rid of all of you to get the rubies and gold. So give me that book."

"Is he talking about the Book of Proverbs?" asked Slidekick.

"That's it," Bo Evil agreed. "The treasure is hidden in that book."

Solomon shook his head sadly. "Bo Evil, you've got it all wrong. The treasure is wisdom that is better than gold. It helps you make right choices. You don't have to steal it. You can read it for yourself."

"A book! It's just a book? Forget it. I don't need wisdom. I'm smarter already than the rest of you put together. Good-bye!"

Mrs. Beaverton hurried up to join them as they watched Bo Evil ride away on his motorcycle.

"That was a close call," said Max.

Slidekick nodded. "You saved my life, Solomon."

"You saved my life first when you rescued me from the river," Solomon added.

"But, how'd you get here so fast?" Slidekick asked.

Solomon answered, "I chose to do the wise thing and live God's way. And God gave me a special gift! He made me supersonic! From now on I'm living my life for the Lord!"

"I'm proud of you, Solomon," said Mrs. Beaverton. "Say, everybody, it's time for the country fair to begin!"

"Yippee!" the three friends yelled.